For Violet and Primrose, my best Christmas presents ever

COPYRIGHT © 2001 by Callaway & Kirk Company LLC.

Nicholas Callaway, President and Publisher
Antoinette White, Senior Editor • Toshiya Masuda, Art Director
George Gould, Production Director • Carol Hinz, Associate Editor
Ivan Wong, Jr. and José Rodríguez, Production • Sofia Dumery, Design
Kathryn Bradwell, Publishing Assistant • Elizabeth Hole, Editorial Assistant
With thanks to Jennifer Rees at Scholastic Press, and to Raphael Shea, Art Assistant, at David Kirk's studio.

Library of Congress catalog card number: 00-131019

ISBN: 0-439-31463-1

10 9 8 7 6 5 4 3 2   03 04 05 06 07

Printed in China
First edition, November 2001

The paintings in this book are oils on paper.

Little Miss Spider

A Christmas Wish

paintings and verse by David Kirk

Scholastic Press

Callaway

New York

B

eneath the green boughs
Of her first Christmas tree,
Sat Little Miss Spider
Alone with her tea.

Reaching out to a star—
She shed a small tear
And wished for the *one* gift
She wanted this year.

With a kiss for her mom
She swung outside to play
Hoping now that a friend
Would be coming her way!

But in the wide woodland
There wasn't a sound.
All the insects were sleeping—
Not a friend to be found.

Then Little Miss Spider
Was knocked on her face.
Asparagus Beetle laughed,
"Get up! Let's race!"

They slid to the river
To glide on the ice
And dash through the snow tunnels
Mined by the mice.

Falling flat on their backs,
They gazed up at the skies
And waved all their arms
To make snow butterflies.

They built a grand castle
From bricks made of snow
With gargoyles guarding
To frighten all foe.

Asparagus rolled out
A carpet of green
To cushion the steps
Of his beautiful queen.

The sun went to sleep,
The great forest turned black.
Miss Spider cried,
"How will I find my way back?"

Asparagus lifted her
Into the night
Guided home through the trees
By the stars' gentle light.

"I must not come in,"
He said with a bow.
"I ought to get home
To my own family now."

The presents were wrapped,
The tree shining bright.
Still, something was missing—
Christmas didn't feel right.

They spotted him curled
In a clearing below,
Lying shivering, alone,
By his family of snow.

And gathering him home
With their family made new,
Two wishes were granted,
Two dreams had come true.

Together they found
All the joy Christmas brings—
With the love of glad hearts
Beneath sheltering wings.